INVESTIGATING

BONES

CRIME SCENE INVESTIGATORS

INVESTIGATING BONES

Ellina Litmanovich and Sara L. Latta

Enslow Publishing
101 W. 23rd Street
Suite 240
New York, NY 10011
USA
enslow.com

Published in 2018 by Enslow Publishing, LLC.
101 W. 23rd Street, Suite 240, New York, NY 10011

Library of Congress Cataloging-in-Publication Data

Names: Litmanovich, Ellina, author. | Latta, Sara L., author.
Title: Investigating bones / Ellina Litmanovich and Sara L. Latta.
Description: New York, NY : Enslow Publishing, 2018. | Series: Crime scene investigators | Includes bibliographical references and index. | Audience: Grades 5-8.
Identifiers: LCCN 2017016485 | ISBN 9780766091825 (library bound) | ISBN 9780766095427 (paperback)
Subjects: LCSH: Forensic anthropology—Juvenile literature. | Victims of crimes—Identification—Juvenile literature. | Criminal investigation—Juvenile literature. | Forensic sciences—Juvenile literature.
Classification: LCC GN69.8 .L57 2018 | DDC 599.9—dc23
LC record available at https://lccn.loc.gov/2017016485

Printed in China

To Our Readers: We have done our best to make sure all website addresses in this book were active and appropriate when we went to press. However, the author and the publisher have no control over and assume no liability for the material available on those websites or on any websites they may link to. Any comments or suggestions can be sent by email to customerservice@enslow.com.

Portions of this book originally appeared in the book *Bones: Dead People Do Tell Tales.*

Photo Credits: Cover and interior pages (skeletal remains) Marques/Shutterstock.com; cover and interior pages (magnifying glass) azure1/Shutterstock.com; pp. 6, 47, 56-57 AFP/Getty Images; p. 8 orxy/Shutterstock.com; p. 9 Mariarita Stefani, Vicenza, Italy/FOAP/Getty Images; p. 12 Menahem Kahana/AFP/Getty Images; p. 13 Marco Di Lauro/Getty Images; p. 15 Anwar Amro/AFP/Getty Images; p. 17 Jodie Adams/Shutterstock.com; p. 20 Press Association/AP Images; p. 25 Old Paper Studios/Alamy Stock Photo; p. 27 FL Historical collection 9/Alamy Stock Photo; p. 29 Chicago History Museum/Archive Photos/Getty Images; p. 34 David Howells/Corbis Historical/Getty Images; p. 37 John B. Carnett/Popular Science/Getty Images; p. 39 © AP Images; p. 42 Arterra/Universal Images Group/Getty Images; pp. 48-49 KRT/Newscom; p. 51 Orlando Sierra/AFP/Getty Images; p. 53 Science Source; pp. 58-59 Louise Gubb/Corbis Historical/Getty Images; p. 62 Millionstock.com/Shutterstock.com; p. 64 Bettmann/Getty Images; p. 66 Robert Nickelsberg/The LIFE Images Collection/Getty Images; p. 71 David Parker/Science Photo Library/Getty Images; p. 72 Steven Raymer/Corbis Historical/Getty Images; pp. 78-79 Bob Daemmrich/AFP/Getty Images; pp. 84-85 Doug Kanter/AFP/Getty Images; p. 87 Nader Khouri/KRT/Newscom; p. 89 John Moore/Getty Images.

CONTENTS

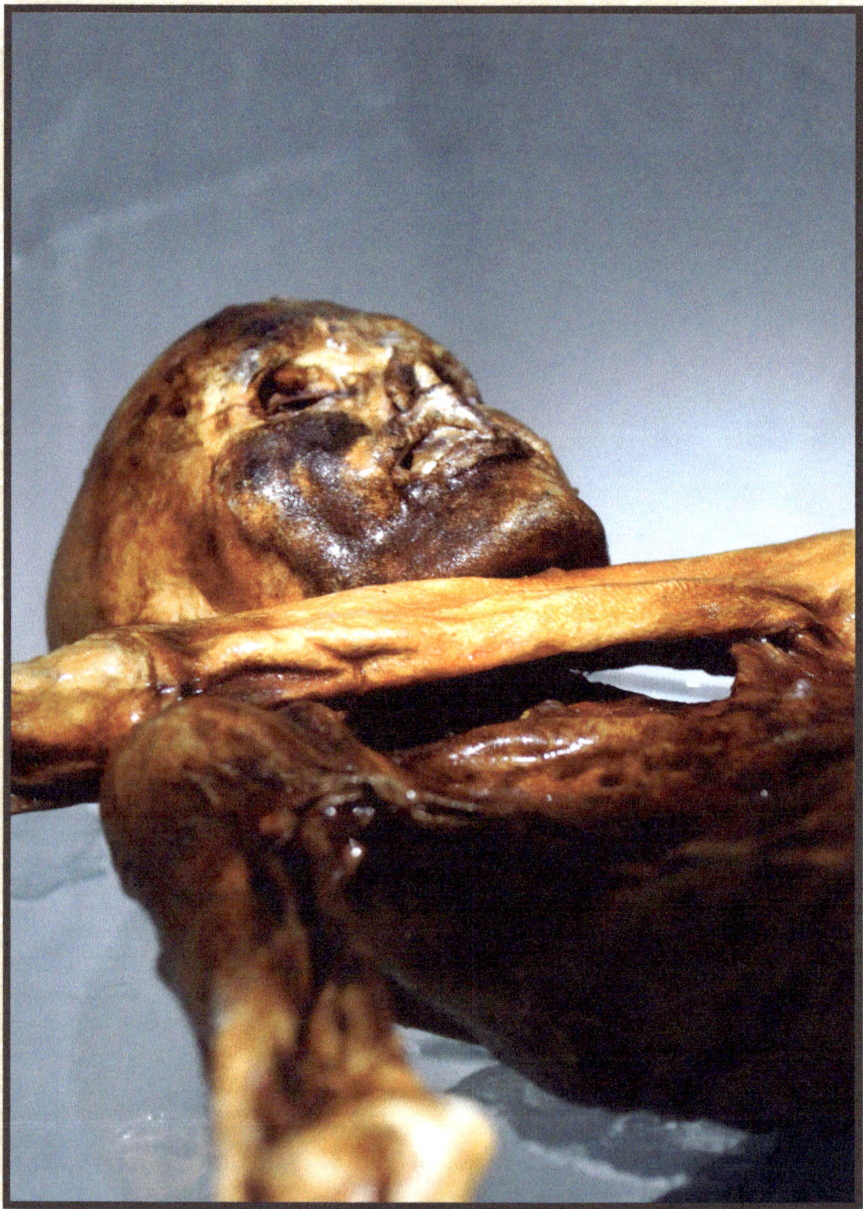

Ötzi, the Iceman, is the oldest known mummy found in Europe. Studying his remains provides valuable information about humans who lived during the Copper Age.

THE ICEMAN

Ötzi, or the Iceman as he's known, is one of the oldest cold cases in history. He was discovered in 1991 by two hikers in the Ötzal Alps, on what is now the Italian-Austrian border. Today one of the biggest questions in forensic anthropology is "Who killed the Iceman?" There are clues to the time period he was from and how he died, but no one can tell who actually did it.

Ötzi, named after the Alps where he was found, lived during the Copper Age (about five thousand years ago). He was somewhere between his late forties and early fifties when he died. His body, clothing, and blood were all preserved by the cold climate of the Alps. He had been lodged between two glaciers, but once global warming began, the glaciers melted and he was found.[1]

A decade after Ötzi was found, Detective Inspector Alexander Horn of the Munich Police Department was asked to look at the body. He was amazed to see how well the body had

This photo shows the glaciers between the Schnalstal and Oetztal valleys. Ötzi, along with some belongings, was discovered on the Schnalstal Valley glacier.

been preserved. Ötzi's demise came from a flint arrow to the back.

Up until 2017, most of what was known about Ötzi was his height, approximate weight, and age. However, with advanced technology, scientists determined that the murder was not a robbery but a personal vendetta. Forensic anthropology also gave light to the fact that Ötzi was probably sick since many of the tattoos he had on his body were on his joints. This meant that the tattoos were marks for acupuncture points. Lastly, it is also now known what Ötzi ate as a last meal: grains and meat from an ibex, a type of wild goat.[2]

The wild alpine ibex lives in the European Alps. Prehistoric humans hunted them for food.

Forensic anthropology is the reason why many cold cases have been reopened in recent times. With the help of modern technology, clues from crime scenes, and the will to find out the truth, law enforcement agencies can finally make sense of all of their evidence.

CHAPTER 1

WHAT IS FORENSIC ANTHROPOLOGY?

Imagine you're out for a walk with your dog. Your dog smells something in the bushes. You go take a look and find a small body part. You call the local law enforcement, and they come quickly. They take photos at the crime scene. They call a forensic anthropologist to identify the body part and how long it's been there.

A forensic anthropologist is a scientist who studies human bones to answer legal questions, often in criminal cases. These experts are called in when local law enforcement and the medical examiner need help solving the case.

Bones Don't Lie

In 2005 Leroy Adams went to live with his son, Lon, after Hurricane Katrina destroyed his New Orleans home. His daughter, Lynne Landreneau, was worried about him. She had

A member of a search-and-rescue team looks for survivors in New Orleans. Hurricane Katrina, which hit Louisiana, Mississippi, and Alabama in August 2005, was one of the deadliest hurricanes in US history.

last seen him during Christmas, but since then, every time she called to talk to him, her brother made up an excuse. Finally, she filed a missing persons report in June 2008.

The deputies searched Lon Adams's home. What they found were remains of someone who had been dead for a while. Detective Todd Giacona said the room had what he called "a Katrina smell: Mildew with a mixture of death."[1] He believed they found Leroy, but the body was so decomposed that the authorities called forensic anthropologist Mary Manhein.

When Manhein and her team arrived on the scene, they took pictures, made notes, and carefully slid a piece of cardboard under the remains and placed them into a body bag. The bag was then taken to their lab.

The shape of the skull and pelvis told them that the remains belonged to a man. The wear and tear of the bones told them that the man was old. The remaining dried-out tissue and bones confirmed that the man had been dead for some time. Dental records confirmed that it was in fact Leroy Adams.

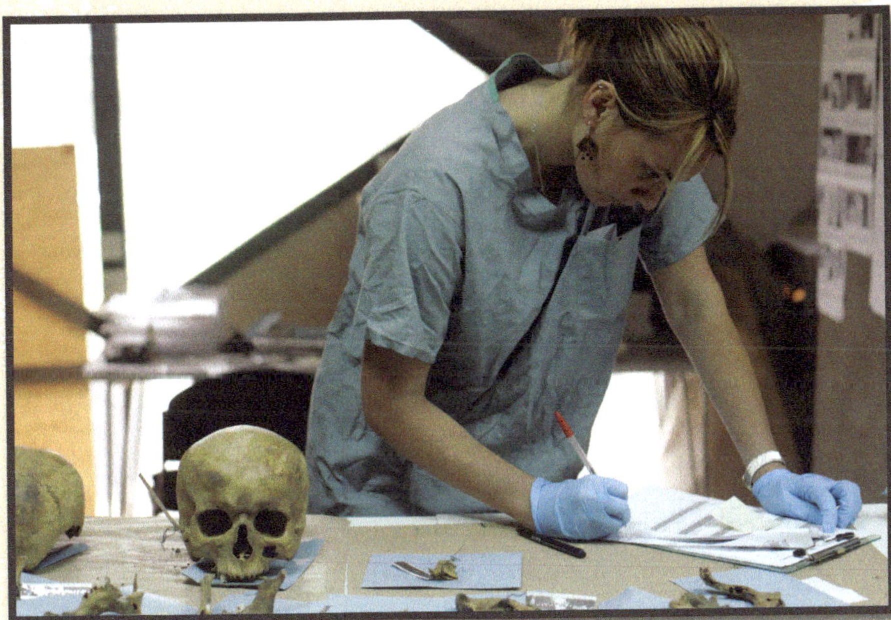

Forensic anthropologists use various pieces of information, such as dental records and DNA samples, to identify remains.

While preparing to X-ray the skeleton, Manhein discovered that the body had been through trauma. There were many broken bones that never had time to heal during his life. Based on all of the evidence, Lon Adams was charged with murder.

At the trial, Adams confessed that he accidentally killed his father. He didn't go to the bedroom where his father died for two and a half years. His attorney argued that the elder Adams fell out of the bed and died. Manhein found that unlikely. Dr. Karen Ross, the medical examiner for the case, said, "In my opinion, I don't see how a fall onto that foot locker would account for all those rib fractures. . . . I think it was intentionally inflicted trauma, either punching or kicking."[2]

In the end, the story the bones told won. The jury found Lon Adams guilty of manslaughter.

What Does a Forensic Anthropologist Do?

When officers discover a body of someone who died from an unknown cause, murder, or suicide, they call a medical examiner or coroner to help investigate. If there was foul play, the investigators will ask a forensic anthropologist to help figure out the who, the when, and the how of someone's death. Many forensic anthropologists have training in archaeology, which makes them valuable.

They help dig up remains, take photographs and soil samples, and look for other tell-tale clues at

An archaeologist carefully works on a skull. Forensic anthropologists may learn archaeological techniques to unearth bodies without damaging them.

the site. They examine insect activity and chemicals around the body to help determine how long the person has been dead. Once the investigators have thoroughly examined the site, they send the bones and remains to a lab for further study.

Whose Bones Are They?

As a forensic anthropologist, your first task is to determine if the bones are human. A biological anthropologist can tell the difference between the bones of animals and humans. You would then have to determine if the remains belong to a male or female. A man has a narrow, tall pelvis while a woman has a wide, shallow pelvis.

The next mystery is age. The answer to that is in the bones. We are born with 300 bones, but as we age, the bones fuse together. By the time we are adults, there are only 206 bones. Because each bone fuses at a predictable rate in most people, the fused and unfused bones can provide valuable clues about the age of the skeleton. For example, the collarbone fuses between the ages of eighteen and thirty, but the bones that join at the base of the skull don't fuse completely until the ages of twenty to twenty-five. So if a skeleton has a fused collarbone but bones that have not yet completely joined at the base of the skull, the individual was probably between eighteen and twenty-five years of age. Teeth are another way of finding out a person's age, particularly in children who have not yet lost all

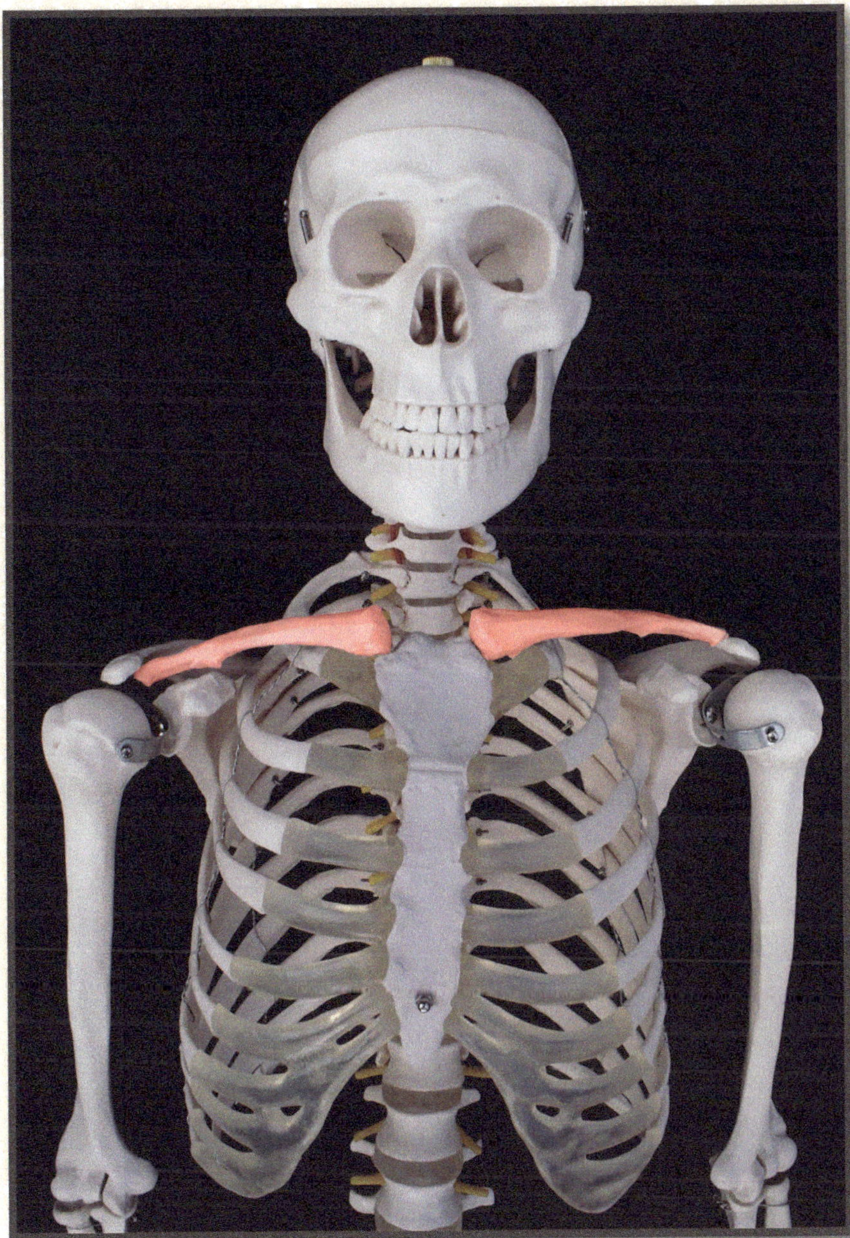

The collarbone, or clavicle, is highlighted in red. Experts can estimate the age of a skeleton by seeing whether or not the collarbone has fused together.

Squirley's Coffin

On June 4, 1959, firefighters in the San Francisco Mountains of southwestern New Mexico discovered a car in flames. They put the fire out and sorted through the wreckage. They found a mass of burned flesh, a skull, some other bones, and a few large teeth.

The car belonged to Armando, nicknamed "Squirley." His brothers-in-law were called in to identify the remains. There was no doubt. The teeth belonged to Squirley.

Squirley's family buried the remains. Some time later, hungry and exhausted, Squirley walked into a logging camp. He told the sheriff that his car had an electrical fire. He had been carrying dynamite caps in his car, so he decided to bail out of the window before it blew up. He hit his head and wandered until he stumbled upon the logging camp.

So who—or what—was buried in Squirley's coffin?

Squirley told the sheriff that in his car he had an old Indian skull, a porcupine, and some calf bones. A bone expert confirmed his story. Squirley kept that coffin in his living room until the time came for him to be buried in it.

Although this story is true, it would never happen today. In the 1950s, law enforcement officials did not routinely call bone experts to examine remains. The discipline of forensic anthropology simply did not exist.[3]

Fortunately, today things have changed.

of their baby teeth. Also, as we age, teeth begin to lose their strength.

Bones in the skull can give clues to an individual's ancestry as well. You can see by looking at your parents that you have inherited traits from each of them. Your height, weight, coloring, and physique can be traced back to one or more of three major world groups: European, Asian and Native American, or African.

You now know the sex, ancestry, age, and height of the person. You can find out who they were from their dental records. You can tell if the individual was working class or white collar. Also, if there were signs of trauma, you now know there was foul play involved.

As a forensic anthropologist, your job is to look for clues that would help you understand what happened postmortem (after death). This is an area of study called taphonomy. Are there animal bite marks? Does the site have insects that could give clues to the death? Insects, climate, chemicals left by the decomposing body, and plant growth in and around the remains all provide clues about what happened to the body after death. For example, flies arrive at the body shortly after death and lay their eggs; beetles and wasps come later.

After you return the bones and evidence, you give officials your take on the matter. If the person cannot be matched through the database, you may work with a forensic artist who will create a clay

A forensic anthropologist demonstrates how a tiger tooth fits the bite mark in a bone from a Roman gladiator, revealing how he may have died.

likenesses of the person directly on a reproduction of the skull itself, or you might take a 3-D X-ray scan of the skull to help you re-create a digital image of the individual. Shown on local television stations, on social media, and in newspapers, these images might prompt someone to come forward and identify the individual. If the case goes to trial, you may be asked to act as an expert witness, where you must be able to back up your testimony with sound scientific data.

William Maples, renowned forensic anthropologist said, "They have tales to tell us, even though they are dead. It is up to me, the forensic anthropologist, to catch their mute cries and whispers, and to interpret them for the living, as long as I am able."[4]

CHAPTER 2

THE BEGINNING OF FORENSIC ANTHROPOLOGY

Little was known about forensic anthropology during the late nineteenth and early twentieth centuries. Many cases were judged incorrectly due to little evidence provided by law enforcement. Multiple murders went unsolved. Examiners didn't have the extensive knowledge that forensic anthropologists have today.

Pay Your Debts

Dr. George Parkman was a wealthy and popular man in Boston, Massachusetts. He spent much of his time overseeing properties and running his money-lending business. But he was very unforgiving when it came to collecting debts. Dr. John Webster, a Harvard professor, was a fun-loving man who was the complete opposite. He was careless and in a lot of debt. They had once been good friends, but that ended after Webster borrowed money from Parkman with no intention of paying it back.

On November 23, 1849, Parkman went to the grocery store. He left his groceries at the store, saying he would come back, and went to collect money from Webster. He never returned.

His worried wife contacted her brother-in-law, and he posted notices of Parkman's disappearance on flyers and in newspapers across the city.

The police questioned Webster, who said that he had indeed met with Parkman. "I paid him the debt I owed," he insisted, saying that Parkman had hurried out of his office soon after.[1] Webster had never really been a suspect, and the police had no reason to doubt him.

Ephraim Littlefield, the janitor, had his own suspicions. He and his wife lived in the basement of the medical college, right next to Webster's laboratory. "He had always been at me like some yapping dog: Littlefield, did you leave the windows open again; Littlefield, have you been playing cards in my room again?"[2] But shortly after Parkman's disappearance, Webster gave Littlefield a Thanksgiving turkey. That had been the first time.

Littlefield decided to do a little investigating. Knowing the building well, he went down to a vault under Webster's office. Webster had the only key to the chamber, so Littlefield hacked through the wall. Peering inside, he saw part of a body hanging from a hook and "a pelvis . . . some pieces of leg . . . Perhaps I was expecting a body; perhaps nothing, but not these bits of butcher's trash sitting on the wet dirt. They were so white, you see, so clean and white."[3]

Littlefield called the authorities. They found a breastbone and ribs hidden in a tea chest. There was a set of false teeth in the oven. They found a burned bone and a button in the furnace. About 150 bones or bone fragments were found scattered throughout Webster's office. That evening, Webster was arrested and charged with murder.

The police called in experts to examine the remains. One of the experts was a professor of anatomy at Harvard, Dr. Jeffries Wyman, who helped piece together Parkman's bones. Another expert was Oliver Wendell Holmes Sr., dean of the Harvard Medical College. The investigators concluded that the remains were clearly those of a human.

At the trial, the testimony of Parkman's dentist and friend, Dr. Nathan Keep, clinched the case against Webster. Keep had made Parkman a pair of dentures four years earlier. Parkman's lower jaw was so unusual that Keep had to make special molds to make the dentures. He had kept the mold, just in case Parkman ever needed another pair of dentures. On the witness stand, Keep showed how the false teeth fit his molds exactly.

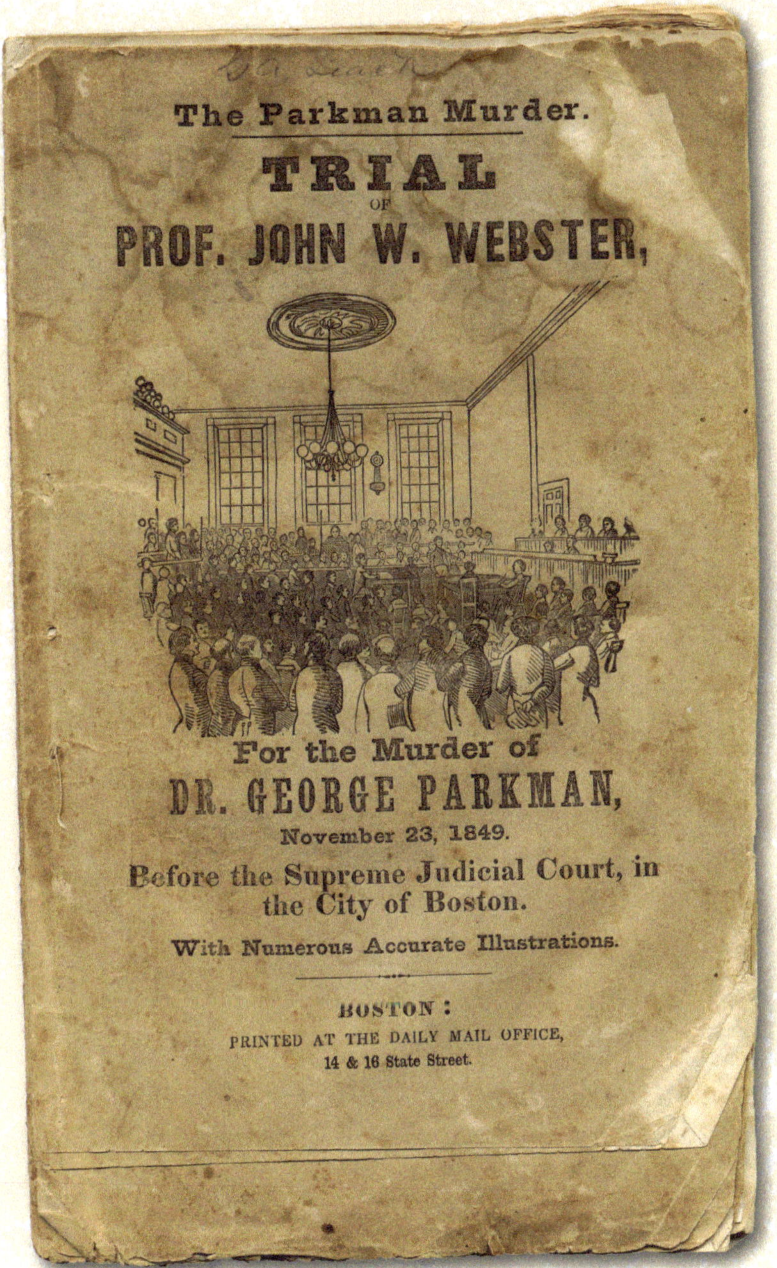

The Parkman Murder.

TRIAL

OF

PROF. JOHN W. WEBSTER,

For the Murder of

DR. GEORGE PARKMAN,

November 23, 1849.

Before the Supreme Judicial Court, in the City of Boston.

With Numerous Accurate Illustrations.

BOSTON:

PRINTED AT THE DAILY MAIL OFFICE,

14 & 16 State Street.

This booklet contains the judicial proceedings of the trial against Dr. John Webster for the murder of Dr. George Parkman.

The Father of Forensic Anthropology

All of Boston was transfixed by the sensational murder trial of John Webster. Thomas Dwight grew up listening to stories about how Parkman's bones helped convict Webster. Dwight went to medical school and devoted his career to the study of anatomy at Harvard. He showed how an expert could determine characteristics such as sex, age, height, or ancestry from just a few bones.

Although Dwight never testified in any high-profile court cases, he wrote a groundbreaking paper, "The Identification of the Human Skeleton: A Medicolegal Study." His research earned him the title of "the Father of Forensic Anthropology."[4] One of Dwight's students was George Dorsey, who would play an important part in another sensational murder case.

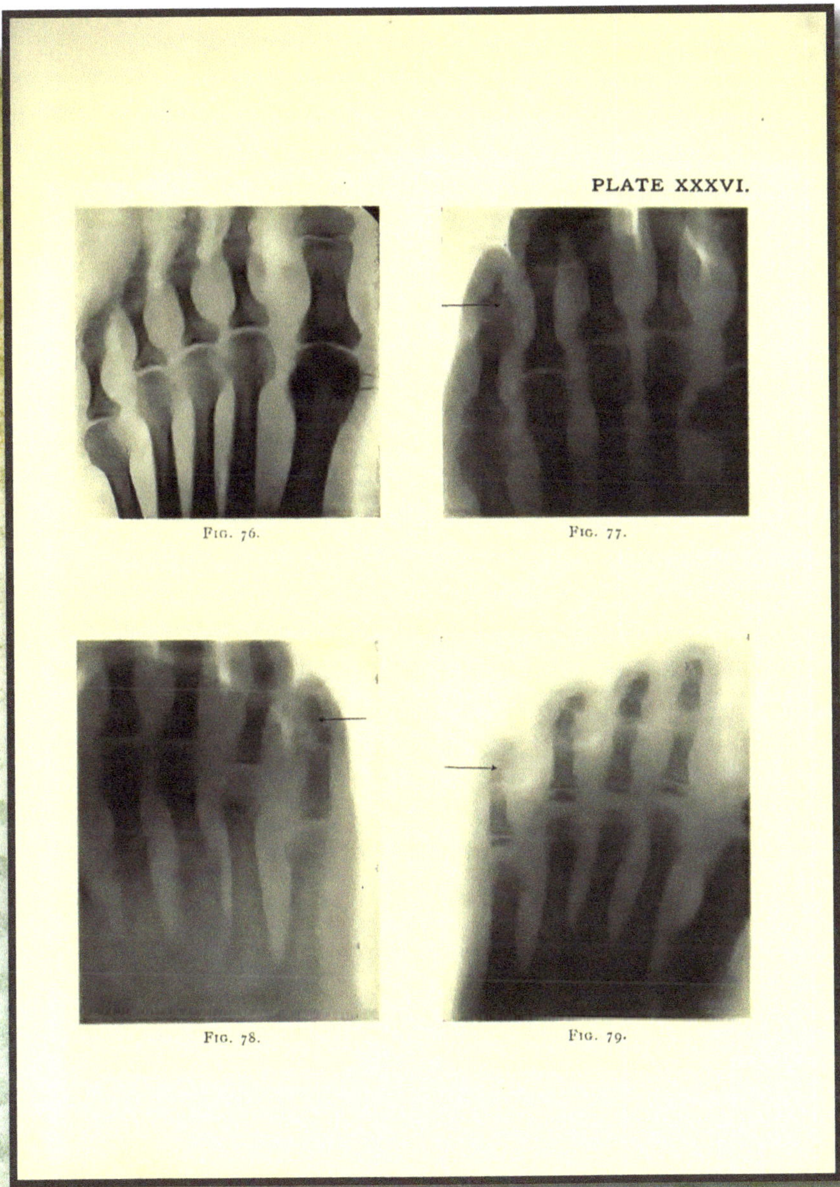

Thomas Dwight took these images to show the variations that exist in the hand and foot bones of different individuals.

Webster was found guilty of murder and sentenced to hang. Before he died, he admitted to killing Parkman by hitting him over the head with a sturdy piece of wood. As his laboratory furnace was too small to burn an entire body, he planned to burn it one piece at a time.

Milestones in Forensic Anthropology

Adolph Luetgert made the best sausages in Chicago. Visitors to the German restaurant during the 1893 World's Fair in Chicago raved about the delicious sausages. Encouraged by his success, Luetgert built a large house and a new sausage factory next door. His wife, Louisa, thought they should be saving their money, but Adolph didn't listen to her.

Adolph had married Louisa sixteen years earlier. He had given her an unusual eighteen-carat gold wedding ring engraved with her initials, "L. L." But from the beginning, their marriage was a stormy one. Not long after the World's Fair, the economy fell. By 1897 Luetgert was in debt and Louisa blamed him for their financial mess. He then began sleeping in the factory.

On March 11, 1897, Adolph ordered 378 pounds (171 kilograms) of potash. Potash, which was commonly used to make soap, is highly acidic. It can burn or dissolve human flesh. On April 24, he ordered two of his employees to empty the potash into barrels alongside a vat in his factory. Later that day, Luetgert and another employee poured

The World's Columbian Exposition of 1893, also known as the Chicago World's Fair, was held to celebrate the four hundredth anniversary of Christopher Columbus's arrival in the New World.

the potash into the vat and filled it with water. It simmered for about a week.

On May 1, Adolph sent his factory watchman on two errands that took him out of the factory. That was the last day Louisa Luetgert was seen alive. Later, neighbors reported seeing Louisa and Adolph going into the sausage factory that night. At first, Adolph told people that his wife had gone to visit her sister.

Six days later, her brother reported her missing to the police, who then searched the factory. They found a huge vat of some greasy, foul-smelling substance. Luetgert explained that it was simply a mixture of chemicals, animal fat, and scraps of animal bones. He'd been trying to make soap to clean his factory, he said.

When the police officers drained the vat, they found a few small bone fragments, a piece of woman's undergarment, and two gold rings.

Adolph Luetgert was charged with murdering and boiling his wife's remains in a chemical solution. With nearly all of her body dissolved into a greasy jelly, how could Luetgert be proven guilty?

At the trial, Luetgert said his wife must have left him because she was unhappy. She would turn up, he was sure. The rings, he said, were too small for his wife's fingers. And the bone fragments? "Laughing heartily until his big cheeks shook," the newspaper report read, "Luetgert held up a fragment said to be a part of his wife's shoulder blade. "'This is a bit of a cow's shoulder bone,'" he said.[5]

Luetgert's defense attorney found witnesses who claimed they had seen Louisa at a railroad station 50 miles (80 kilometers) away. The jury could not come to a decision, so the judge dismissed them and called for another trial.

In the second trial, both sides brought in bone experts. W. H. Allport, professor of anatomy at Northwestern University Medical School, testified for the defense. Allport said that there was no way of identifying any of the bones as human. He confidently said that one of the bones was definitely from a hog. The lawyer for the prosecution decided to test Allport's knowledge of bones. He pulled some bones out of a paper bag and asked Allport to identify them. Allport examined the bones for about ten minutes. They had belonged to a dog, he said.

No, he was told. He'd been examining the arm and hand of a monkey. "Well, it might be a dog monkey," Allport retorted. "They look a good deal alike."[6] After that, poor Allport began to fall apart. After a while, he kept answering, "I don't know."

One of the experts for the prosecution was George A. Dorsey, a curator at the Field Museum in Chicago. Dorsey was the first person to graduate from Harvard with a doctoral degree in anthropology. He had spent his career studying ancient human remains and was considered an expert in determining a skeleton's sex.

The case came down to four bone fragments so tiny that all of them would fit on a quarter. The bones, Dorsey said, were a piece of a bone from her hand, a bit of rib, and parts of bones from her toe and foot. All of them, he said, had undoubtedly come from a human female. So convincing was he that those four tiny bones, along with the wedding ring and the suspicious circumstances surrounding Louisa's disappearance, were enough to convince the jury. Luetgert was sentenced to life in prison. He died of a heart attack in prison a year later, still protesting his innocence.

The Luetgert case marked an important milestone for forensic anthropology. It was the first legal case in which an anthropologist was called upon to testify as an expert witness.

CHAPTER 3

SOLVING MYSTERIES

To solve the mystery of "who did it," a forensic anthropologist needs to understand how the body works. Before forensic anthropology became popular with law enforcement, medical examiners made many mistakes. They didn't realize that several different factors affected how bodies decomposed. But thanks to people who wanted to fix mistakes of the past, there is now a laboratory that examines these factors and their impact on remains.

The Body Farm

Just a few miles from downtown Knoxville, Tennessee, there are bodies that lie buried in shallow graves, submerged in ponds, or stuffed into the trunks of cars. Some are crawling with maggots, swathed in the sickly sweet smell of decaying flesh. Others are little more than a pile of dry bones and a mat of hair.

It's not the scene of a crime, but the University of Tennessee Anthropological Research Facility, also known as the Body Farm. All corpses were donated to the Body Farm by the families of the dead for scientific research. Students and scientists come to learn more about what happens to a human body after death.

Postmortem

Immediately after death, the body begins to cool down to the temperature of its surroundings. A few hours after death, chemical changes in the muscles cause the body to stiffen. Enzymes begin

A body decays at the Body Farm. Up to eighty bodies at a time are left to decompose under a variety of circumstances for scientific research.

to break down cells in the body. Eventually, tissue turns to liquid and the body begins to break down from bacteria.

Once the body fluids begin to seep into the soil and the corpse dries out, mites and other beetle species begin to move in. Eventually, after the enzymes, bacteria, various types of insects, and perhaps scavenging animals have done their work, all that remains is a dry pile of bones. The entire decomposition process can take as little as two weeks in a warm climate or much longer in a cold climate. Climate and soil conditions can slow down or even stop the decaying process.

After studying the decomposition of hundreds of bodies, scientists at the Body Farm came up with a mathematical formula that uses weather data at the crime scene to calculate time since death with great accuracy.

The Headless Corpse

The Body Farm came about because of an incident while identifying human remains. In 1977, Dr. Bill Bass, a well-respected forensic anthropologist for the state of Tennessee, got a phone call from Detective Jeff Long. Someone had dug up the grave of Colonel William Shy, a Civil War soldier. Inside the coffin lay a fairly recent deceased headless corpse. Investigators suspected that the body of Colonel Shy had been stolen and replaced before the murderer could finish burying the new body.

After examining the cadaver, Dr. Bass concluded that the victim had been dead for no more than a year, yet further investigation revealed that the body was in fact Colonel William Shy. Tissue analysis concluded that the soldier's body had been embalmed, and his cast iron coffin had been sealed so tightly that it kept out the insects and bacteria that cause decay. Grave robbers had dug up his remains for relics. Dr. Bass had misjudged the time since death by more than a century![1]

Dr. Bass realized that he and other forensic scientists understood very little about what happens to the human body after death. What effect do climate and weather have on the rate of decomposition? What can the insects in and around the body tell us about the time since death? Pathologists cannot perform a normal autopsy on bodies that have already begun to decompose, so forensic anthropologists are there to answer those questions.

Dr. Bass decided that forensic anthropologists needed a laboratory to conduct experiments on their subjects. The University of Tennessee gave him an acre of land near the campus. In 1981, Dr. Bass built a simple storage shed and a strong security fence around his acre, and he then laid a donated corpse on a concrete slab, thus creating the Anthropological Research Facility.

Since then, Dr. Bass and his colleagues have studied the decomposition of bodies under a wide range of conditions. They bury the bodies in shallow graves in the woods, stuff them in the trunks of cars, or submerge them in water. They write down everything that happens to the body. Dr. Bass's goal was to create a sort of decomposition database. "Any time a real-life murder victim was found, under virtually any circumstances or at any stage of decomposition, I wanted to be able to tell police—with scientific certainty—when that person was killed," Bass said.[2]

Students, professors, police officers, and FBI agents have all come to the Body Farm to learn more about what happens to the human body after death.

Dr. William Bass founded the Body Farm to learn what happens to bodies postmortem in order to provide more accurate information to investigators.

Determining Cause of Death

It is not always possible for a forensic anthropologist to determine how someone died. The bones of an old man who died peacefully in his sleep reveal nothing about his final moments. But forensic anthropologists are very good at reading the clues to trauma that damages bones. Blunt-force trauma—most commonly occurring as a result of an automobile accident—is the fifth most common cause of death in the United States. But it is also the type of trauma most often seen when somebody has been murdered. Baseball bats, tire irons, and frying pans may leave a distinctive imprint on the victim's bones that is a sure giveaway to forensic anthropologists.

Knives or machetes cause sharp-force trauma. Anything with a cutting edge will slice through bone, leaving behind clean edges. A broken hyoid bone, a tiny horseshoe-shaped bone in the throat, almost always means that the victim was strangled to death. A bullet to the skull may leave characteristic entry and exit holes. The size and shape of the holes are clues to the type of gun used and at what range it was fired.

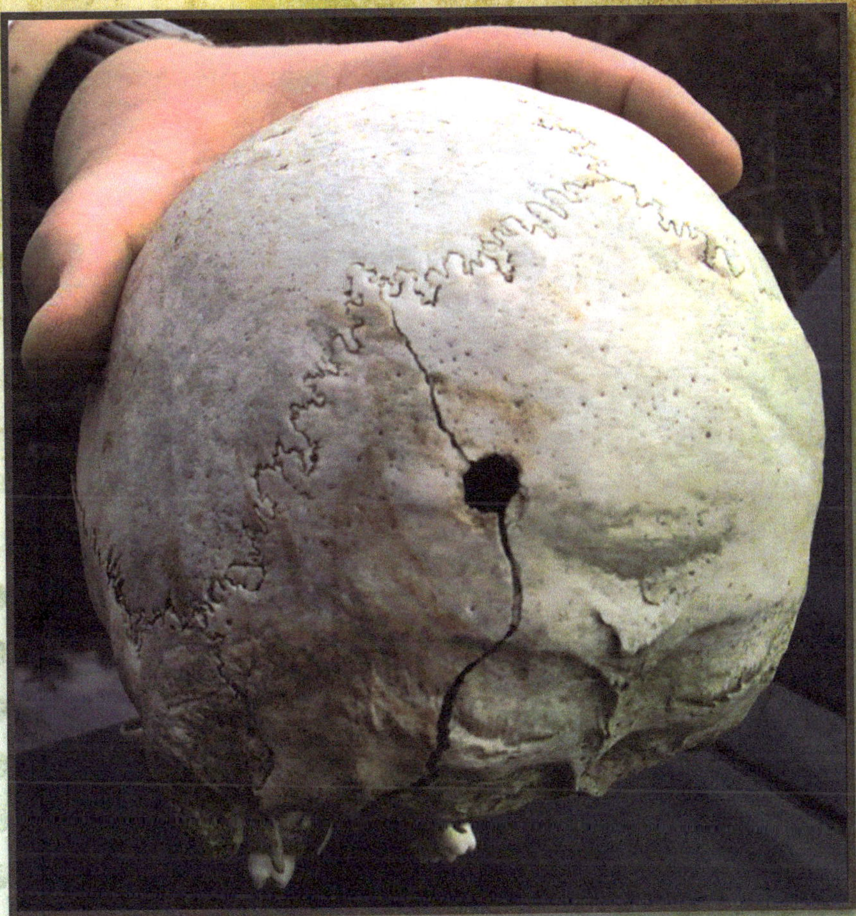

This skull has a bullet hole in the back, which experts believe was caused by a small-caliber gun. They also believe that the shooting was not accidental and that the young woman had been dead for at least five years.

Insects Tell a Story, Too

By 1999, Dr. Bass had been studying bodies at the Body Farm for nearly twenty years. He and his colleagues had carried out experiments on the decomposition of more than three hundred corpses under every imaginable condition. That year he got a call to help solve a case in which establishing time of death was critical. By this time, he was confident that he was up to the challenge. He was soon going to find out just how difficult that would be.

On November 5, 1993, Darrell and Annie Perry and their young daughter Krystal left New Orleans for a much-needed getaway. The couple had been having problems and wanted time to sort things out. Darrell's stepfather, Mike Rubenstein, had offered to drive them to his secluded cabin nearby. Mike had checked on the cabin twice in the month of November, he said, but both times it was dark and locked.

On December 16, he found the bodies of Darrell and Annie lying on the living room floor while Krystal's body lay on a bed in the next room. All three of the bodies were already badly decomposed, bloated, and crawling with maggots. The medical examiner determined that Darrell and Annie had been stabbed to death; Krystal had been strangled.

Lead investigator Allen Applewhite discovered that Rubenstein had filed a life-insurance claim for a quarter of a million dollars on his four-year-old granddaughter only twenty-four hours later. Applewhite learned that Rubenstein and Darrell's mother had taken out the $250,000 policy on their granddaughter two years earlier, which had kicked in three months prior. There was a clear motive, but no hard evidence. No fingerprints, footprints, bloody knife—nothing. The district attorney refused to prosecute the case.

But the memory of the little girl and her parents haunted Applewhite. He found that two of Rubenstein's acquaintances had also come to mysterious ends and both times, he benefited from their deaths. Finally, in 1999, Applewhite convinced the district attorney's office to prosecute Rubenstein for the murders. The case went to trial in June of that year.

Rubenstein had an airtight alibi for the two weeks before the bodies were found. If the defense could prove that the family had been alive during that period, then Rubenstein would go free. Establishing the time of death was critical. The chief witnesses would be the maggots found on the bodies of the victims.

Applewhite sent Dr. Bass detailed photographs of the bodies. All three were in an advanced stage of bloat. Since timing of the decomposition process can vary according to the climate, Dr. Bass asked for the temperatures between November and December of 1993. Based on the data, Dr. Bass found that the family had been killed sometime

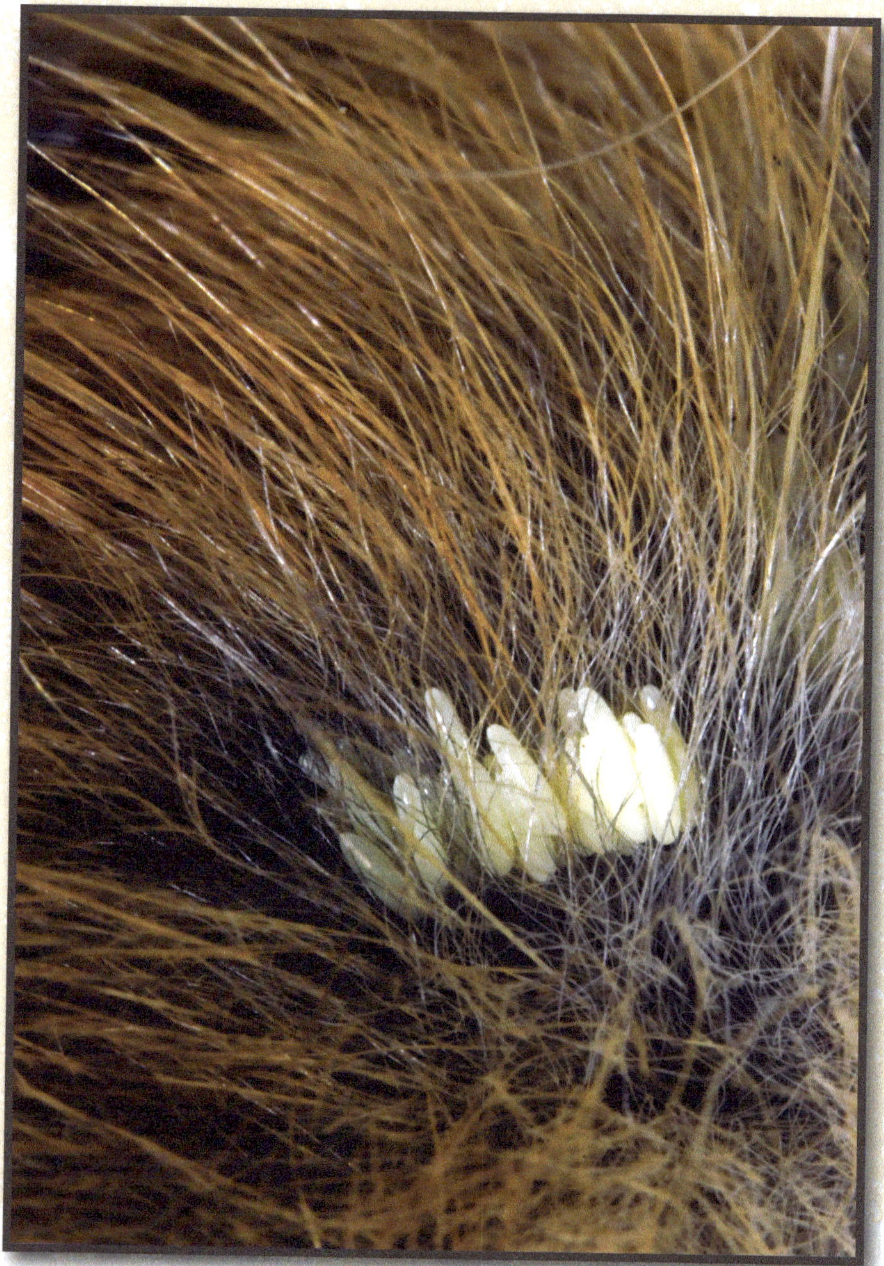

These are greenbottle fly eggs in the fur of a dead squirrel. Forensic anthropologists can use the life cycle of insects to determine time of death.

between twenty-five and thirty-five days before they were found—mid-November.

But something puzzled him. The maggots in the photos appeared to be in the third and final growth stage before turning into pupae. This meant that they would have hatched from eggs about two weeks earlier. He didn't see any empty pupa casings, either. The maggots could only tell him that the murders had happened at least two weeks before the bodies were found—December 2.

At the trial, Dr. Bass acknowledged that the maggot story didn't quite fit with the decomposition story. The cabin was tightly built, so it would take the maggots time to find a way in. He worried as the trial continued. Finally the maggot pupae made an appearance. A pathologist from the county medical examiner's office took the stand for the defense. She showed a close-up photo of Krystal's face and head. Dr. Bass had never been shown these photos—and what he saw stunned him. "You've got to stop this trial," he whispered to the prosecuting attorney. "You've got to put me back on the stand."[3]

The enlarged photo clearly showed empty pupa casings scattered amid the roots of the girl's hair. It was clear that the blowflies had begun laying their eggs more than two weeks before the bodies were discovered. Krystal and her parents were already dead by December 2—the earliest date for which Rubenstein had an alibi.

Forensic Data Bank (FDB)

After a research project is completed, the scientists clean the bones, measure them, and enter all of the information about the bones into the Forensic Data Bank (FDB). The scientists also input any other information they have about the individual, such as birth place, age at death, medical history, and occupation. The database contains information on more than 4,080 cases from the United States, Central America, South America, Europe, and Asia.[4]

The data bank is the heart of a computer program called FORDISC (Forensic Discrimination), the world's leading database of modern human skeletons. A forensic anthropologist can enter a few skeletal measurements from an unknown crime victim and the software can estimate the ancestry, sex, and height of the person.

The jury found Rubenstein guilty of three counts of first-degree murder. He received a sentence of life in prison for the murder of Darrell and Annie, and a death sentence for the murder of Krystal. In October 2009, the Mississippi Supreme Court overturned the death penalty because a judge had failed to tell the jurors they could have sentenced Rubenstein to life without parole. He is now serving a sentence of three life terms.[5]

CHAPTER 4

CRIMES AGAINST HUMANITY

History shows us that human cruelty knows no bounds. We have heard multiple stories of the great genocides of the Armenians, Jews, Syrians, and Ukrainians, as well as other groups who didn't agree with the government where they lived. Some bodies were burned while others were dumped in unmarked graves. Thanks to forensic anthropology, these graves can be excavated and the bones identified, and the victims' families can finally get closure.

The Junta

In 1976, in Argentina, military rulers seized power. The country was in great turmoil. After the election, the new ruling body, or Junta, vowed to restore order to the country. The "Dirty War" expanded from political enemies to anyone who disagreed with their policies.

This 1976 photo shows the three leaders of the Argentine military dictatorship called the Junta on the day they deposed President Isabel Perón: from left to right, Admiral Emilio Eduardo Massera, General Jorge Rafael Videla, and Brigadier-General Orlando Ramón Agosti.

Thousands of men, women, and children were kidnapped and taken to detention centers, where they were often tortured or killed.

The Junta were left with the problem of getting rid of the bodies. Some were returned to their families. These victims, the Junta claimed, had killed themselves. Some of the victims were drugged and dumped from airplanes into the shark-ridden waters. Others were buried in "No Name" (NN) graves. As far as the Junta were concerned, bones were bones. All of these people came to be known as *desaparecidos*, or "disappeared ones." For their families, it was as though they had vanished.

The Dirty War ended in late 1983, when Argentina elected a new president, Raúl Alfonsin. "Today public immorality has ended," Alfonsin said at his inaugural address. "We are going to build a decent government."[1] He pledged to investigate the disappearances and punish those responsible. Alfonsin formed a commission to investigate the fate of the disappeared ones. Six months later, the commission released a report with the names of 8,961 desaparecidos and a list of

In 2003, a group of forensic anthropologists uncovered more than 120 victims of the Junta's Dirty War in a mass grave in Cordoba, Argentina.

the military officers believed to be involved in the disappearances.

Judges ordered hundreds of NN graves to be dug up. With little knowledge or skills in forensic anthropology, workers used bulldozers and shovels to dig up NN graves. Human rights lawyers knew that it would be impossible to recover any useful forensic evidence from the piles of jumbled and broken bones. They needed forensic experts to help with the exhumations. They did not trust Argentine forensic experts because some had worked with the Junta. They needed someone from the outside.

That person was Clyde Snow. Snow was one of the leading forensic anthropologists in the United States. He had helped piece together charred bodies and victims of serial killers, and had put names to fallen soldiers. If anyone could read the stories of the bones of the disappeared ones, it was Snow.

Clyde Snow managed to find a group of students who were interested in helping identify the disappeared. Most of them had no experience. Snow and his team began to work as Argentine police and the family of a woman believed to be buried in the NN grave looked on.

The team carefully excavated the grave just as they would a prehistoric site. When they reached the skull, it was marked by a bullet-sized hole. "While she was still in the ground," Snow said, "This woman was telling us she had died of a gunshot wound."[2]

They identified the body from dental records. The remains were not those of the woman in question, but the judge was still impressed. Snow soon flew back to the United States. He returned the following year with a second team. Snow showed

Forensic anthropologist Clyde Snow holds a skull he found in El Maguelar, Honduras. He helped identify the remains of the desaparecidos buried in the mass graves.

these students how to recover, clean, and preserve bones, as well as how to read them.

Dr. Lowell J. Levine, a forensic dentist, taught the students how to compare a victim's teeth with dental records and X-rays made before death. Forensic pathologist Robert H. Kirschner showed them how to recognize the different types of gunshot wounds and evidence of torture. Forensic radiologist John Fitzpatrick taught the students how X-rays could be used to help identify victims.

Over the course of the workshop, the scientists and students exhumed the remains of several disappeared ones. One of them would forever change the way that we investigate human rights violations.

Justice Granted

Liliana Pereyra was twenty-one years old. She lived in Mar de la Plata, Argentina. A free spirit, she was part of a student organization that opposed the Junta. In October 1976, a witness saw two men in military uniforms grab Liliana and her boyfriend Eduardo and shove them into waiting cars. Liliana was five months pregnant.

Nine months after the kidnapping, Liliana's mother, Coche Pereyra, received a notice from the police. Her daughter had been killed in a shoot-out with the military. She had been buried in an anonymous grave. No further information was given. A fellow prisoner who made it out alive told Coche that her daughter had been tortured at a secret detention center before giving birth to a baby boy. After that she had disappeared.

When President Alfonsin was elected, Coche began her own investigation. With the help of a lawyer, she discovered that two women had been buried in NN graves in July 1978. She believed that one of them was her daughter. Coche heard

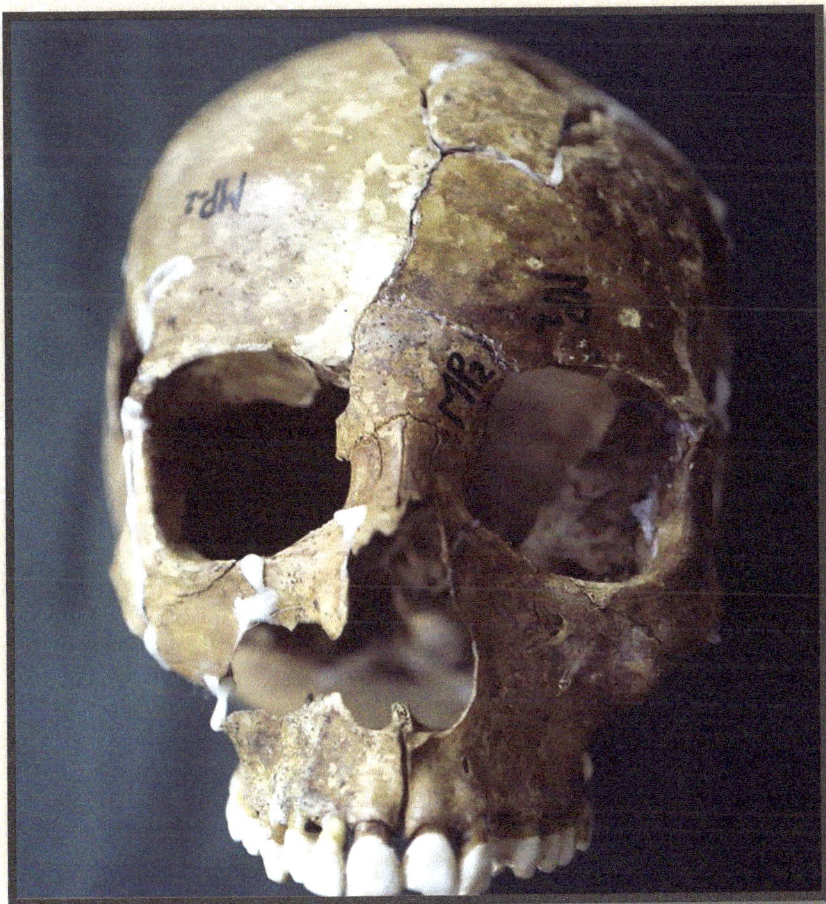

Clyde Snow and his team found and reconstructed the skull of political prisoner Liliana Pereyra.

there was a group of forensic scientists who could possibly help.

In March 1985, Snow, the scientists, and students unearthed a grave. For two weeks they studied the bones. They determined that the bones had belonged to a young woman of European ancestry about Liliana's height. Levine, the dentist, found that she had had one of her canine teeth removed. They reassembled the shattered skull. Kirschner, the pathologist and an expert in gunshot wounds, could tell by the pattern of the fracture indicated that she had been shot at close range.

Although Liliana was pregnant at the time she was abducted, there were no fetal bones inside of this skeleton. A distinctive groove in the pelvis showed that the woman had most likely given birth. The clincher was in the X-rays of the skeleton. Just as no two fingerprints are alike, no two bones are exactly alike. Fitzpatrick, the radiologist, compared X-rays of the bones with those taken of Liliana before her abduction. They were a perfect match.

In May 1985, nine members of the Junta were brought to trial on a total of 711 charges of kidnapping, torture, and murder. This would be the first time that military leaders would be tried for past human rights abuses. Snow was a witness for the prosecution. Using slides to illustrate his testimony, Snow showed how they had determined Liliana's identity and cause of death. He explained how the bones showed that she was killed at close range by a single bullet. Ending his testimony with a photograph of Liliana before her death, he said, "What I would like to point out here is that in many ways the skeleton is its own best witness."[3]

Ultimately, the court sentenced two of the defendants to life in prison. Three others received terms of four and a half to seventeen years. Four were found not guilty.

The Future of Argentine Forensics

After the trial of the Junta was over, the group of students who helped with the investigation became full-time researchers, forming the Argentine Forensic Anthropology Team. They continued their work of documenting human rights abuses in Argentina. Soon, the team's accomplishments began to attract the attention of human rights organizations in Guatemala, El Salvador, and other Latin American countries where similar crimes had taken place. They helped investigate massacres and trained teams of scientists in how to use the forensic techniques Clyde Snow and his team had taught them. Eventually, they would be called upon to help investigate crimes against humanity all over the world

Seeking Justice

Clea Koff's fascination with bones goes back to her childhood, when she would bury bodies of birds found near her home, only to dig them up later to see how long it took them to "turn into" skeletons.[4]

Abuelas Take Action

Knowing that her grandson was probably still alive, Coche Pereyra joined a group, Las Abuelas de la Plaza de Mayo (Grandmothers of the Plaza de Mayo). They took their name from the place where they gathered for years along with the mothers of the disappeared to protest and demand that their loved ones be returned. These women were determined to track down and recover the babies kidnapped

from the desaparecidos. They combed through birth certificates and adoption papers, acted on anonymous tips, and hired investigators to find the missing children. When DNA testing became available, they compared the DNA of the grandmothers with the DNA of children suspected to have been among those kidnapped. Since 1977, the grandmothers have found 113 missing babies.

At a press conference in Buenos Aires, Argentina, on August 22, 2014, Las Abuelas de la Plaza de Mayo joyfully announce that a baby kidnapped during the Dirty War, and whose parents were murdered, was found.

When Koff was eighteen years old, her father gave her a book that set her on the path to forensic anthropology. The book was called *Witnesses from the Grave: The Stories Bones Tell*, which relates the story of Clyde Snow and the Argentine Forensic Anthropology team.

When the president of the African nation of Rwanda was killed in a plane crash in 1994, members of the ruling Hutu party launched an all-out, well-planned slaughter of the minority Tutsi people and Hutus who opposed the campaign. Although the two tribes had lived side by side and shared a common culture for centuries, tensions between the two populations had worsened in recent years. Goaded on by the governing party and driven by fear, soldiers and civilians alike massacred their Tutsi neighbors. Almost one million Tutsis, as well as Hutus who opposed the campaign, had been killed.

Koff was in graduate school and studying forensic anthropology when she watched the news reports on television. "Who's going to go over there and identify all those bodies?" she asked herself.[5] Less than two years later, she joined a United Nations team of archaeologists, anthropologists, pathologists, and others to do just that. The goal was to

A young child looks at the skulls of Tutsis and Hutus that were massacred in Rwanda. Clea Koff was a member of a team sent to help identify the bodies.

identify the bodies. It was done to document that the victims had been murdered so that prosecutors could bring those responsible to trial.

Over the course of two missions to Rwanda, Koff and her colleagues excavated and analyzed the remains of hundreds of victims. Barely a week after returning home from her second mission to Rwanda, Koff left for Bosnia. A civil war in this eastern European country had left thousands of people from opposing ethnic groups dead. She dug up bodies, many of them civilians.

Koff was able to carry out her grisly job, she said, by concentrating on the notion that she was helping provide critical evidence for the international trials where the authorities in Rwanda and Bosnia had been charged with genocide and crimes against humanity.[6]

CHAPTER 5

SEEKING ANSWERS

Some cases may take a lifetime to solve, if they are solved at all. By then, it may be too late to bring the perpetrator to justice. Many of these cold cases go back years, decades, or even centuries, but they are still discussed today. Sometimes the bones give you answers right away. Sometimes they stay silent for a long time.

The Angel of Death

Prisoners at Auschwitz-Birkenau, the World War II Nazi concentration camp, had a name for camp doctor Josef Mengele: the Angel of Death. Survivors recall a handsome man standing on a platform, whistling an opera tune as he inspected the new arrivals. With a flick of his hand, he waved the majority of them to the left—toward the gas chambers. The remainder would be put on work detail—or be forced to take part in his medical experiments.

This is the main entrance to the Auschwitz-Birkenau concentration camp, where Josef Mengele inflicted unimaginable horrors upon the prisoners.

Mengele had been trained as an anthropologist before becoming a medical doctor and was very interested in heredity and genetic differences. Like Adolf Hitler, Mengele believed in the superiority of "Aryans," their name for "pure-blooded" Germans and northern Europeans who were typically tall, blond-haired, and blue-eyed. Mengele and the Nazis believed that Jews, Roma (commonly called Gypsies), other ethnic groups, and those with mental or physical disabilities were substandard human beings.

Mengele performed experiments on his subjects. Those who did not die from the procedures themselves were often killed afterward so that he could dissect and study their bodies. "He believed you could create a new super-race as though you were breeding horses," said Martina Puzyna, a prisoner at Auschwitz who also happened to be an anthropologist. "Man is so infinitely complex that the kind of strict control over such a vast population could never exist . . . He was mad about genetic engineering . . . I believed that he would have killed his own mother if it would have helped him."[1]

By the time the Russians liberated Auschwitz on January 27, 1945, Mengele had fled—but not before collecting two boxes of papers relating to his "research." American troops captured him later that year. Not knowing that he was a notorious war criminal, they freed Mengele. For several years, he laid low in the German countryside, even as some of

Josef Mengele managed to evade capture for his war crimes.

his fellow Nazis were being tried and put to death for war crimes. Mengele became one of the most wanted men in Europe.

In 1949, after years of living under a false identity, Mengele boarded a ship to Argentina. For three decades he feared discovery, so his health faltered. In February of 1979, he went for a swim in the ocean and drowned. Mengele was buried as Wolfgang Gerhard.

The hunt for Mengele continued. People claimed to have sighted him all over the world. The German and Israeli governments offered large rewards to anybody who found Mengele. Finally, in 1985, the West German police uncovered evidence that Mengele was buried in a Brazilian cemetery. Many thought that it was an elaborate hoax. Simon Wiesenthal, who had gained fame as a Nazi hunter, was skeptical. "This is Mengele's seventh death," he said. "Only in Paraguay has he been dead three times, always with witnesses who say it is him. On one of these occasions, we found the body of a woman."[2]

The curious gathered to watch as gravediggers labored to unearth the body believed to be Mengele's. They smashed the lid of the coffin with a pick. In an image that would be broadcast on television sets throughout the world, a member of the Brazilian police department picked up the skull and held it high for all to see. Then, the skull and the rest of the bones were casually dumped into a white plastic tub and taken to a laboratory, where they remained under armed guard.

Clyde Snow was watching the evening news when the grisly scene appeared on his television set in Oklahoma. "They're making a carnival show out of this," he muttered to himself.[3]

Snow knew that the police officers, untrained in forensic techniques, could easily botch such an investigation and he said so on a broadcast the following day. He joined teams of forensic scientists from the United States, Brazil, and West Germany to study the remains. The atmosphere was tense; Snow's comments had stung the Brazilian investigators. They knew that the eyes of the world were on this case.

Investigating the Bones

The forensic scientists had some physical information on Mengele. His records described him as a white male, 5 feet 8 inches (174 centimeters) tall. His dental chart showed that he had twelve fillings. He was right-handed. Also, while at Auschwitz, he had been involved in a motorcycle accident, although the records didn't indicate that he had broken any bones. It wasn't much to go on—but it was all they had.

The scientists gathered around the table where the bones had been laid out by the Brazilian investigators. Richard Helmer, a West German skull expert, shook his head when he saw the skull—perhaps the most critical piece of evidence. It lay in pieces, smashed by the gravedigger's shovel. Only the top part of the cranium was intact.

An international team of forensic scientists examined the bones thought to belong to Josef Mengele.

Helmer, using tweezers, glue, and seemingly endless patience, worked on reconstructing the broken parts of the skull. Snow and the other forensic scientists focused on the remaining bones. Judging from the sturdy bones of the cranium and the narrow pelvis, they knew their skeleton was male. The shape of his skull suggested that he was of European ancestry. But they still had to rule out whether the bones had in fact belonged to the real Gerhard, Mengele's assumed identity.

Judging from the wear and tear on the teeth and bones, the man had been between sixty and seventy years of age when he died. Gerhard would have been in his fifties in 1979. The length of his femur indicated that he was 5 feet 8 inches tall. Gerhard was more than 6 feet (183 cm) tall. Whoever was buried in Gerhard's grave, it was definitely not Wolfgang Gerhard himself.

A team of forensic radiologists and dentists made another important discovery. An X-ray of the skull's upper jaw revealed a curiously wide gap between the two halves of the upper palate—a sign that the man had had a gap between his two front teeth. This gap-toothed trait is an inherited condition found in just 11 percent of the world's population. The scientists glanced between the X-ray and a photograph of Mengele at the age of twenty-seven, his smile clearly revealing the gap between his two front teeth.

Helmer took just three days to assemble the pieces of the shattered skull. He then glued in ten teeth and a set of dentures found in the grave. He studied the skull—the size of the eye sockets, the angle of the cheekbones, the width of the nasal opening. The bone structure underlying faces is what allows us to recognize individual faces, and Helmer had recently perfected a technique that would allow him to compare a skull with a photograph.

He secured pins with a dab of clay to thirty points on the skull. He mounted it on a post next to a photograph of Mengele taken in 1938. Helmer focused one video camera on the skull, and a second one on the photograph, fiddling with both images until they were the same size. Then, he superimposed the two images.

The normally calm Helmer excitedly summoned the rest of the forensic scientists. The photograph was perfectly superimposed onto the skull, every point matching. The team was sure that the skull belonged to Josef Mengele, but many others remained unconvinced. Finally, investigators located a dentist in Brazil who had treated a man named Wolfgang Gerhard in 1978 who matched Mengele's description. The dental X-rays matched those of the skull perfectly.

Identifying Missing Warriors

The year was 1972, and the United States had been at war with North Vietnam for thirteen long years. Captain Anthony Shine, a US Air Force fighter pilot, was flying his aircraft on a military patrol mission near the border of Laos and North Vietnam when he radioed his wingman, another pilot flying nearby. He was going to move down below the cloud cover for a closer look, he told the wingman.

The wingman waited. After ten minutes had passed, he tried to radio Shine. There was no word. Had Shine been shot down? Ejected from his plane, possibly to be captured by the enemy? A search-and-rescue team carried out a two-day search, but Shine was never found. The thirty-three-year-old Shine was declared missing in action, leaving behind a wife and three young children in New York State.

The Joint POW/MIA Accounting Command (JPAC), the military unit charged with finding and identifying missing warriors, says that nearly 84,000 Americans remain unaccounted for since World War II. More than 1,700 of these were involved in the Vietnam War.[4] Based on the island of Oahu in Hawaii, JPAC scientists and investigators send out search-and-recovery teams all over the globe to find the remains of missing service members. JPAC's Central Identification Laboratory is the largest forensic anthropology lab in the world.[5] This is where the mystery surrounding Captain Shine would finally be solved.

Although the Vietnam War ended in 1975, it would be decades before US investigators were allowed to search for the bodies of the missing service members. In 1994, a team from the United States and Vietnam followed a tip that the body

DNA FINGERPRINTING

Although the investigators involved in the Mengele case concluded the remains in Wolfgang Gerhard's grave were indeed Mengel's, some Israeli authorities remained unconvinced. In 1990, the German prosecutor in charge of the case turned to British scientist Alec Jeffreys, the father of an amazing new technique called DNA fingerprinting. Although more than 99 percent of DNA material is identical in all humans, a small number of sequences are unique to each individual. These are called DNA fingerprints. By comparing two different DNA samples, scientists could determine whether they came from the same person, related people, or unrelated people

DNA in bones tends to break down over time. Jeffreys compared the DNA samples from the bones with those of Mengele's son. The results were clear: the son was related to the man whose bones they'd unearthed. The forty-year-old war crimes investigation was finally closed.[6]

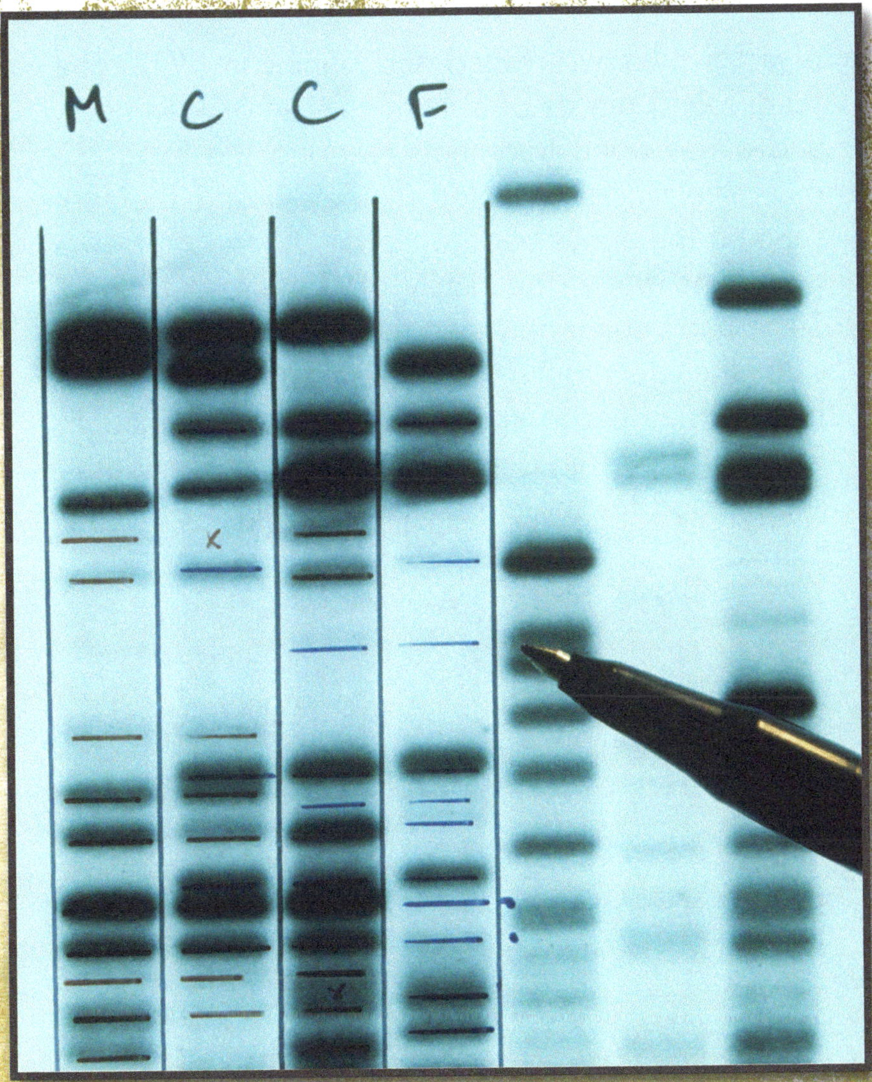

This image shows the bands of a DNA sample. The DNA fingerprints marked "M" belong to the mother (in dark red), the ones marked "C" belong to two children, and the bands with the "F" are the father's (in blue). Both of the children share a few of the bands with each parent, which proves their relationship.

of a US pilot was found and buried in 1972. The team found pieces of a flight suit, an oxygen hose, and a few bone fragments. Lacking the expertise of a forensic anthropologist, they closed the site, sending the bones back to Hawaii.

All the while, the family of Lieutenant Colonel Shine had been monitoring the search. Not satisfied with the government's efforts, Shine's daughter flew to Vietnam to conduct her own investigation. Renting a jeep and hiring a Vietnamese translator, she headed for the crash site. She found a villager

A ceremony is held at Hanoi's No Bai International Airport in 1994 for the remains of GIs killed during the Vietnam War before being sent to Hawaii to be identified.

who had her father's helmet—complete with Captain Shine's name written on the inside. This evidence was enough to send another recovery team back to the crash site. This time, they talked to the man who had found Shine's helmet. The plane, he said, had been shot down. The pilot had ejected from his seat before crashing. They found the dead pilot in a tree and buried him in an old bomb crater nearby.

The site was a gold mine of information: more bone fragments, the pilot's dog tag, and pieces of his flight suit. The forensic anthropologist at the site was careful to document and preserve each piece of evidence. This was important because it was not uncommon for some Vietnamese to "plant" more recent remains in old craters, hoping to be paid for their efforts. But photos taken at the site showed live, unbroken rootlets growing into the pilot's bones—proof that the remains had been in the ground for a very long time.

But how could they be sure the bone fragments were actually the remains of Lieutenant Colonel Shine? Since the remains were so small and so few, the forensic anthropologists at the Central Identification Laboratory in Hawaii analyzed the mitochondrial DNA (mtDNA) in the pieces of bone. They compared the mtDNA from the bone fragments with the mtDNA from Lieutenant Colonel Shine's mother, brother, and sister. They found that the longest mtDNA sequence they got from the bone samples matched Lieutenant Colonel

Shine's relatives. It was found to occur in less than 4 percent of samples from unrelated people—not a perfect match, but given all of the other evidence, good enough.

Lieutenant Colonel Shine was buried, with full military honors, at Arlington National Cemetery. Colleen Shine was satisfied. "The scientific evidence of these few fragmentary remains, coupled with the aircraft wreckage and circumstantial evidence, offered our family long-awaited peace of mind and heart. My mother now knew that she was no longer a wife but a widow, and my brothers and I knew that our father was not being tortured, and that he would never walk back into our lives. Dad died doing something he loved, flying, and for a cause in which he believed."[7]

What Is mtDNA?

The DNA that resides inside the nucleus of every cell is what makes each person unique and is widely used for DNA fingerprinting. But DNA is easily destroyed. It breaks down over time. It is often difficult to recover DNA from old bones or from remains that have been burned.

However, not all DNA resides in the nucleus. Some DNA is also found in the mitochondria, the parts of the cell that serve as power generators. Mitochondrial DNA exists for one thing only: to tell mitochondria how to do their jobs. And, since it has only one job to do, it is much smaller than nuclear DNA.

But mtDNA is very useful to forensic scientists, for two reasons. First, it is very plentiful: there are thousands of copies of mtDNA for every copy of nuclear DNA. So there is often enough mtDNA left in old bones long after nuclear DNA has dropped to undetectable levels. And while nuclear DNA is a combination of genes from the individual's mother and father, mtDNA comes from the mother alone. This means that a mother and her children, the mother's sisters and her children, the mother's mother—all of the maternal relatives—will share the same mtDNA.

Today, the Central Identification Laboratory uses mitochondrial DNA analysis in more than half its cases.[8]

CHAPTER 6

IDENTIFYING VICTIMS OF DISASTERS

From bombings to airplane crashes, disasters have always wreaked havoc on civilization. As technology advances, so do the schemes and weapons used by terrorists who wish to inflict maximum damage on innocent populations. After the smoke clears and the live victims are rescued, forensic anthropologists must then perform the difficult task of identifying the remains of those who did not make it out so their families can put their loved ones to rest.

Oklahoma City Bombing

On the morning of April 19, 1995, in Oklahoma City, Oklahoma, the Alfred P. Murrah Federal Building was buzzing with hundreds of office workers and visitors. Children in the building's day care center were playing and eating a morning snack. At 9:02 a.m., a van loaded with a huge bomb exploded just outside the building. Super-hot gas streaked through the building. The ground shook in a tremor that could be felt 30 miles (48 km) away. The nine-story building collapsed, creating a crater 30 feet (9 meters) deep.

Minutes later, paramedics, firefighters, and police officers began to arrive on the scene. "In an awful way, it was breathtaking," recalled Jana Knox, an emergency medical technician. "There was glass shimmering on the streets and scrap metal everywhere."[1]

Firefighters worked feverishly to free survivors trapped in the debris. "In about fifteen minutes," Knox said, "our ambulance was almost stripped of supplies. People needing help were everywhere. I would just finish with one and turn around to find twenty more. It was like a scene out of hell, and it would be like this for hours."[2]

By the end of the day, more than eight hundred people had been treated for injuries. One hundred sixty eight people lost their lives. Nineteen of the dead were children. A team of volunteer recovery specialists worked twelve-hour days over weeks to find and identify all of the bodies and body parts buried in the rubble. They wanted to identify all of the victims so that their remains could be returned to their families, of course, but it was also important that they recover every scrap of evidence that might be used to solve the crime.

On April 19, 1995, the Alfred P. Murrah Federal Building in downtown Oklahoma City was bombed by two domestic terrorists.

Agents with the Federal Bureau of Investigation who saw the crater knew almost immediately that they were dealing with a crime scene. A cash machine video camera near the building had captured an image of a yellow moving truck parked

in front of the building just before the explosion. Agents found pieces of the truck, coated with tell-tale traces of the bomb-making material. Soon, agents found an axle from the truck that had held the bomb; an identification number led them to a rental agency in Junction City, Kansas.

A man who went by the name of Robert Kling had rented a van there on April 17. Several people said they had seen a second man with Kling. Using information from people who had seen them, an FBI artist quickly drew up sketches of Kling and his companion—John Doe No. 1 and John Doe No. 2. The agents took the sketches door-to-door in Junction City. They hit pay dirt at the Dreamland Motel, where the manager said that John Doe No. 1 had stayed there and checked out the day before the bombing. But his name wasn't Kling. It was Timothy McVeigh. And he had been driving a yellow moving truck.

Two days after the bombing, a nationwide computer search showed that a twenty-seven-year-old man named Timothy McVeigh was in jail in Oklahoma. He had been arrested ninety minutes after the bombing on a traffic violation. He had posted bond and was scheduled for release in less than an hour. Formal charges were filed against McVeigh for murder, conspiracy, and the destruction of government property.

McVeigh hated and mistrusted the government and had ties to antigovernment groups. These groups, often heavily armed, believe the government threatens their freedom. At the time he was arrested, he was wearing his favorite T-shirt, bearing the image of a tree dripping with blood. Police also arrested and charged McVeigh's friend Terry Nichols. They did not think he was John Doe No. 2—Nichols had been hundreds of miles away when the mystery man had been spotted with McVeigh. But they had ample reason to suspect that Nichols had helped McVeigh plan the bombing.

Rescue workers recovered the last three bodies from a massive pile of rubble on May 29. But they also found something puzzling: part of a decomposed leg, a leg that didn't seem to belong to any of the bodies they'd recovered.

Forensic experts initially thought that the leg belonged to a white male, but they weren't certain. The foot wore two dark socks and a black combat boot. The leg had been separated from the rest of the body about 6 inches (15 cm) above the knee. Pieces of plastic embedded in the bone told them that the victim had probably been very near the center of the blast. Judging by the size of the bone, it might have belonged to a powerful woman or an average size man. Because the leg had been badly damaged from the blast and had lain in the rubble for several weeks, the skin had begun to decompose and discolor. The color told the investigators little about the person's ancestry.

The FBI sent hair and tissue samples to experts in Washington, DC. There, they concluded that the individual was probably female and black, although they couldn't be certain.

Timothy McVeigh's defense lawyer found out about the mystery leg that summer. He accused the experts of lying about their findings to help win the government's case against McVeigh. The leg, he said, must have belonged to the real bomber—John Doe No. 2, who had been described by witnesses as a muscular white man with dark hair.

Doug Ubelaker, the FBI's top forensic anthropology consultant at the Smithsonian Institution, had an idea. He called a forensic anthropologist named Emily Craig, who had written a scientific paper showing that the structure of the knee could yield important clues about the race of an individual. Dr. Craig, who was a medical illustrator before becoming a forensic anthropologist, had long known that the knees of black people have more space at the hinge than those of white people. She had watched thousands of knee surgeries on athletes of all racial groups and had dissected hundreds of amputated legs. If anybody could determine the race of this victim, it would be Dr. Craig.

"I spent a grueling but satisfying day examining every inch of the leg, analyzing tissues, measuring x-rays, and taking detailed handwritten notes," Dr. Craig wrote.[3] At the end of the day, she told the investigators that the leg had belonged to a woman of African ancestry.

The FBI soon confirmed that the leg belonged to Lakesha Levy. She had been buried with someone else's left leg—an understandable mistake given the terrible mutilation of the many body parts that had to be sorted through.

Although the identity of the leg that was mistakenly buried with Levy remains unidentified, Dr. Craig and the medical examiners on the case have confirmed that it belonged to a white female.

Whether that white female was one of the victims somehow buried without her left leg or an unidentified 169th victim remains unknown. What is known is that it did not belong to John Doe No. 2—if he existed.

On June 2, 1997, the jury found Timothy McVeigh guilty of the murder of 168 people. He was executed by lethal injection on June 11, 2001. His coconspirator, Terry Nichols, was sentenced to life in prison for his part in the bombing.

The 9/11 Terrorist Attacks

On September 11, 2001, the Islamic terrorist group al-Qaeda carried out four coordinated attacks against the United States. Two hijacked airplanes crashed into the north and south towers of the World Trade Center in New York City, causing them to collapse less than two hours later. A third airplane flew into the Pentagon in Virginia, and a fourth plane headed to Washington, DC, went down in Pennsylvania after the passengers tried to regain control from the hijackers. Nearly three thousand people died and more than six thousand others were injured in the attacks.

Richard Gould, an anthropologist and archaeologist at Brown University in Providence, Rhode Island, visited the site of the 9/11 terrorist attack on the World Trade Center three weeks after the tragedy. Dr. Gould's trained eyes saw what the cleanup crews could not: human bone fragments among the ashy grey deposits that still covered much of Lower Manhattan. Human remains, office paper stained with blood, and other material were blown far away from Ground Zero—some as far away as Brooklyn, several miles away.

Dr. Gould knew that he could bring his skills as an archaeologist to help find the remains of people who died in the World Trade Center attack. He formed a volunteer group, the Forensic Archaeology Recovery team, to search for material related to the 9/11 attack.

Rescuers remove a body from the rubble of the World Trade Center, September 17, 2001. Forensic scientists would help identify the remains of the victims.

"Four-and-a-half years later, they were still finding human remains in great numbers," he told a reporter. "I'm afraid they may keep finding this material for years."[4]

Disaster archaeology can be very difficult, but Gould knows that the work is invaluable. "Archaeology . . . eventually leads to what is sometimes

called 'emotional closure,' when the victims' remains are returned to their families," he wrote. "Then, that terrible cloud of uncertainty is lifted, and they can begin to grieve."[5]

After the September 11, 2001, attacks on the World Trade Center and the Pentagon and the crash of United Airlines Flight 93 in Pennsylvania, the government called for disaster mortuary operations teams (DMORT) nationwide to help local authorities locate and identify the dead. Working twelve-hour shifts, the team members sorted through the debris, searching for human remains—often very small—and other evidence that might help identify the victims. They sent the remains to laboratories, where forensic anthropologists measured and X-rayed the bones, searching for clues about the victims. Forensic dentists examined the teeth, documenting fillings or wires from braces that might be matched to dental records. They extracted DNA from the remains and compared their samples with blood samples from relatives. They compared their samples with DNA extracted from hair left in combs back home, toothbrushes—anything that might help identify victims.

Paul Sledzik, who headed the DMORT team that worked at the crash site of United Flight 93 in Pennsylvania, summed up the feelings of his team. "It's heart-rending work, absolutely," he said.

Disaster Mortuary Operations Team (DMORT)

It seems that the world has suffered a rash of disasters in recent years. Some, like the bombing of the Murrah Building, are deliberate acts of terrorism. Accidents or natural disasters—airplane crashes, factory explosions, earthquakes, hurricanes, and tsunamis—can claim the lives of hundreds or even thousands in a matter of minutes.

When disaster strikes, the first priority is to save lives. But when the emergency medical teams have done all they can to help save the living, others must find and identify the dead—and that can be a staggering job. The sheer number of fatalities and destruction can overwhelm local medical examiners or coroners.

Fortunately, the specially trained group of volunteers who come together as DMORT can respond to such catastrophes. Forensic anthropologists join specialists in forensic dentistry and pathology, fingerprint experts, photographers, X-ray technicians, funeral directors, medical examiners, and others to identify the victims and investigate the scene. It is a critical job, both for legal reasons and to help grieving friends and families claim the bodies of loved ones.

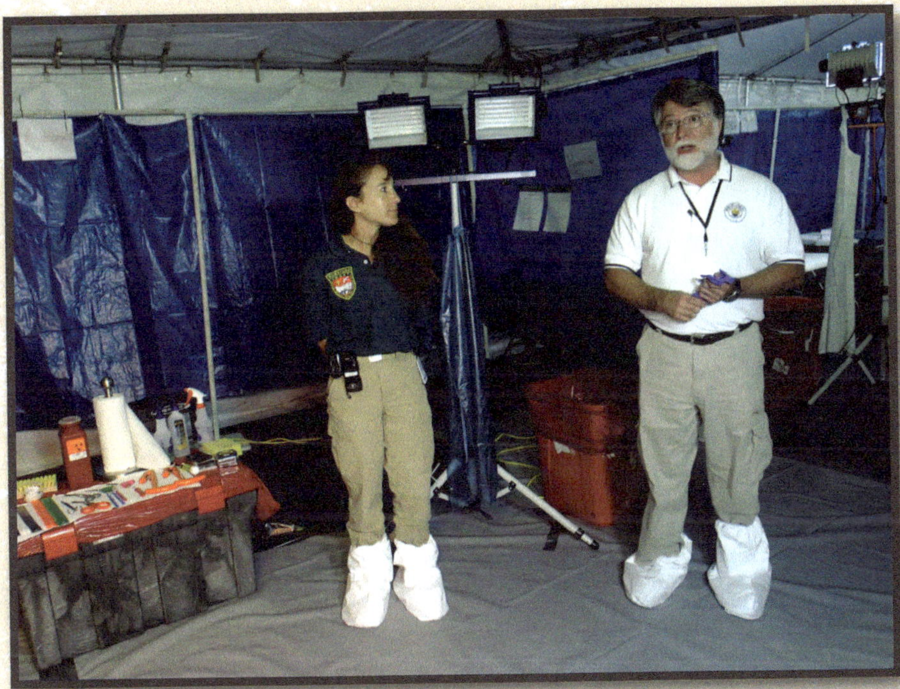

Dr. Corrine Stern (*left*) and Dr. Louis Cataldie give a tour inside the DMORT base camp in Louisiana. This team identified remains of Hurricane Katrina victims.

"But this [DMORT operation] has a distinct difference to it. Given what's been going on nationally, people here are extremely focused on completing the work here. They feel they can provide a service to these families and to their country and they are here to do that."[6]

Career Information

So now you are thinking about becoming a forensic anthropologist. Maybe your interest was sparked by television shows such as *NCIS*, *CSI*, and *Bones*. Unfortunately, being a forensic anthropologist isn't as glamorous as those shows make it out to be. There are sights and smells that most people would not be able to handle. But you are not like other people, and you can most definitely handle it.

To become a forensic anthropologist, you need a bachelor's degree in anatomy, chemistry, or anthropology. You will then have to get your master's degree in human biology or anthropology. To qualify for a career as an investigator, most forensic anthropologists will need to have a PhD as well. Since this career has few positions available, the higher your degree, the better the chance of finding a job in the forensics field. A good accredited school could also open doors for you in the field through classes, internships, and working with local labs. The following are some selected schools offering training in forensic anthropology and related fields:

Forensic anthropology students examine the exhumed remains of immigrants who died crossing the border into Texas in order to return them to their families.

Anthropology Department
California State University, Chico

400 West First Street
Chico, CA 95929-0400
Phone: 530-898-6192
www.csuchico.edu/anth/index.shtml

Applied Forensic Sciences
Mercyhurst University

501 East 38th Street
Erie, PA 16546
Phone: 814-824-2000
www.mercyhurst.edu/ridge-college-intelligence-studies-and-applied-sciences/applied-forensic-sciences

Archaeology and Forensics Laboratory
University of Indianapolis

1400 E. Hanna Avenue
Indianapolis, IN 46227-3697
Phone: 317-788-3486
archlab.uindy.edu/

Department of Anthropology, Forensic Science, and Archaeology
Baylor University

One Bear Place #97173
Waco, TX 76798-7173
Phone: (254) 710-4084
www.baylor.edu/anthropology/doc.php/230528.pdf

Department of Anthropology, Forensic Anthropology Center
University of Tennessee, Knoxville

250 South Stadium Hall
Knoxville, TN 37996-0760
Phone: 865-974-4408
web.utk.edu/~fac/

Forensic Anthropology
University of Florida, Gainesville

Turlington Hall, Room 1112
PO Box 117305
Gainesville, FL 32611
Phone: 352-392-2253
anthro.ufl.edu/about-us/department-subfields/biological-anthropology/forensic-anthropology/

Forensic Anthropology
University of North Carolina, Wilmington

601 South College Road
Wilmington, NC 28403-5907
people.uncw.edu/albertm/

The salary of a forensic anthropologist who teaches at a university can range from $35,000 to $95,000 per year. If you work part-time, you will be making on the lower end of the salary. If you work as a full-time professor at a major university, you will be making much more. Those who work in the federal or state sector, your salary will be based on the experience you have and may range from $75,000 to $95,000 or more.[1] The US Army's Central Identification Laboratory employs forensic anthropologists to search for and recover war casualties. Other forensic anthropologists work for museums, the FBI and state bureaus of investigation, and medical examiner offices.

Forensic anthropologists with training in archaeology often help law enforcement officials recover human remains from crime scenes. They may use their knowledge of soil, plants, and insect activity to help solve the case. Some forensic anthropologists specialize in creating computer or clay models of faces based solely upon a skull.

Although there are no data available for the specific area of forensic anthropology, according to the US Bureau of Labor Statistics (BLS), the mean annual wage for anthropologists and archaeologists is $66,440 and employment is expected to grow 4 percent until 2024.[2]

If you want a career that is exciting, fulfilling, and rewarding, then forensic anthropology may be the right path for you.

CHAPTER NOTES

INTRODUCTION: The Iceman

1. Sarah Pruitt, "Cracking the World's Oldest Cold Case," *NationalGeographic*, March27,2017. http://www.history.com/news/cracking-the-worlds-oldest-cold-case.
2. James Owen, "5 Surprising Facts About Otzi the Iceman," *National Geographic*, October 18, 2013. http://news.nationalgeographic.com/news/2013/10/131016-otzi-ice-man-mummy-five-facts/.

CHAPTER 1. What Is Forensic Anthropology?

1. Paul Purpura, "Detective Recalls Odor of Death; Metairie Man Accused of Killing His Father," *Times-Picayune* (New Orleans), September 23, 2009, METRO, p. 1.
2. Michelle Hunter, "Grandson Testifies He Thought Smell in House Where Grandfather Was Decomposing Was 'Dead Rats,'" *Times- Picayune* (New Orleans), September 24, 2009. http://www.nola.com/crime/index.ssf/2009/09/chad_adams_whose_father_lon.html.
3. Stanley Rhine, *Bone Voyage: A Journey in Forensic Anthropology* (Albuquerque, NM: University of New Mexico Press, 1998), pp. 1–3.
4. William R. Maples, PhD, and Michael Browning, *Dead Men Do Tell Tales: The Strange and*

Fascinating Cases of a Forensic Anthropologist (New York, NY: Doubleday, 1994), p. 280.

CHAPTER 2. The Beginning of Forensic Anthropology

1. Christopher Joyce and Eric Stover, *Witnesses from the Grave: The Stories Bones Tell* (Boston, MA: Little, Brown & Co., 1991), p. 47.
2. Simon Schama, *Dead Certainties: Unwarranted Speculations* (New York, NY: Alfred A. Knopf, 1991), p. 122.
3. Schama, p. 135.
4. T. D. Stewart, *Essentials of Forensic Anthropology* (Springfield, IL: Charles C. Thomas Pub., 1979), p. xii.
5. Robert Loerzel, *Alchemy of Bones: Chicago's Luetgert Murder Case of 1897* (Urbana, IL: University of Illinois Press, 2003), p. 125.
6. Loerzel, p. 170.

CHAPTER 3. Solving Mysteries

1. William Bass and Jon Jefferson, *Death's Acre: Inside the Legendary Forensic Lab—the Body Farm—Where the Dead Do Tell Tales* (New York, NY: G.P. Putnam's Sons, 2003), pp. 59–71.
2. Bass and Jefferson, p. 238.
3. Bass and Jefferson, p. 252.
4. Forensic Anthropology Center, University of Tennessee, "Research," n.d., http://fac.utk.edu/.

5. *Times-Picayune* staff writers, "Marrero Native on Mississippi Death Row Spared Lethal Injection by Supreme Court," October 7, 2009, NOLA.com, http://www.nola.com/crime/index.ssf/2009/10/marrero_native_sitting_on_miss.html.

CHAPTER 4. Crimes Against Humanity

1. Gabriela Nouzeilles and Graciela Montaldo, *The Argentine Reader* (Durham, NC: Duke University Press, 2002), p. 477.
2. Jeff Guntzel, "'The Bones Don't Lie': Forensic Anthropologist Clyde Snow Travels Continents to Bring the Crimes of Mass Murderers to Light," *National Catholic Reporter*, July 30, 2004, pp. 13–16.
3. Christopher Joyce and Eric Stover, *Witnesses from the Grave: The Stories Bones Tell* (Boston, MA: Little, Brown & Co., 1991), p. 268.
4. Clea Koff, *The Bone Woman* (New York, NY: Random House, 2004), p. 8.
5. Koff, p. 15.
6. Jane Perlez, "A 'Bone Woman' Chronicles the World's Massacres," *New York Times*, April 24, 2004, p. 4A.

CHAPTER 5. Seeking Answers

1. Gerald L. Posner and John Ware, *Mengele: The Complete Story* (New York, NY: McGraw-Hill Book Co., 1986), p. 43.
2. Posner and Ware, p. 318.

3. Christopher Joyce and Eric Stover, *Witnesses from the Grave* (New York, NY: Little, Brown and Co., 1991), p. 161.
4. Joint POW/MIA Accounting Command, FY 2009 Annual Report, pp. 3–5, http://www.jpac.pacom.mil.
5. Dawnie Wolfe Steadman, ed., *Hard Evidence: Case Studies in Forensic Anthropology* (Princeton, NJ: Prentice Hall, 2003), p. 109.
6. Nick Zagorski, *Proceedings of the National Academy of Sciences*, "Profile of Alec J. Jeffreys," 103 (24), June 13, 2006, p. 8920.
7. Steadman, p. 288.
8. Central Identification Laboratory. http://www.jpac.pacom.mil/

CHAPTER 6. Identifying Victims of Disasters

1. "The Story of the Oklahoma City Bombing," *The Official Record of the Oklahoma City Bombing, April 19, 1995, Oklahoma Today Magazine*: 2000 revised edition, p. 14.
2. "The Story of the Oklahoma City Bombing," p. 21.
3. Emily Craig, *Teasing Secrets from the Dead* (New York, NY: Crown Publishers, 2004), p. 236.
4. Lucy Middleton, "Laid to Rest at Last," *New Scientist*, March 22, 2008, p. 42.
5. Richard Gould, "9/11: A Disaster Redefines the Meaning of Archaeology," *Dig*, February 2007, p. 9.

6. Cindi Lash, "Flight 93 Victim Identification Long, Arduous," *Pittsburgh Post-Gazette*, September 25, 2001. http:/www.post-gazette.com/headlines/20010925sledzik0925p3.asp.

Career Information

1. Radek Gadek, "Forensic Anthropologist Career, Salary, and Training Information," *Criminal Justice Degree, College, and Career Blog*, January 17, 2016. http://criminaljusticeonlineblog.com/forensic-anthropologist-career/.
2. Bureau of Labor Statistics, US Department of Labor, Occupational Employment Statistics, **"Occupational Employment and Wages, May 2016, 19-3091, Anthropologists and Archeologists."** https://www.bls.gov/oes/current/oes193091.htm.

GLOSSARY

anthropology The science of the origin, development, and culture of humans.

archaeology The study of past human life through the excavation of sites and the artifacts and other physical remains left behind.

autopsy The examination of a body to find out the cause of death.

Copper Age The time period between the Neolithic Age and Bronze Age, marked by the use of copper tools.

coroner A public official whose chief duty is to discover the cause of death, especially one that might not be due to natural causes.

decompose To decay.

detention center An institution that detains those suspected of crimes or illegal status or for political reasons.

DNA fingerprinting The use of DNA to match genes in a forensic sample.

enzyme A protein that originates from living cells that can bring about or speed up chemical reactions.

expert witness A person who is qualified in his or her field to provide a testimony at a legal proceeding.

forensic artist An artist who draws, sketches, or modifies an image for a legal proceeding or to help law enforcement.

genocide The mass slaughter of a group of people because of religious, national, or racial prejudice.

medical examiner Someone appointed by the city who is trained in the medical field and can perform autopsies to investigate crimes.

mitochondrial DNA (mtDNA) DNA that is found in the mitochondria of cells. These genes are inherited only though the female line.

pathologist A medical doctor who specializes in the causes and effects of diseases or of injuries to the body.

pupa The third stage of the life of an insect, between the larva and adult stages.

taphonomy The study of what happens to organisms after they die.

vendetta A prolonged and bitter feud involving vengeful acts.

FURTHER READING

Books

Gardner, Robert, and Joshua Conklin. *Experiments for Future Forensic Scientists.* New York, NY: Enslow Publishing, 2017.

Heos, Bridget. *Blood, Bullets, and Bones: The Story of Forensic Science from Sherlock Holmes to DNA.* New York, NY: Balzer & Bray, 2016.

Innes, Brian. *Forensic Science.* Broomall, PA: Mason Crest, 2016.

Rauf, Don, and Judith Williams. *Forensic Science Specialists.* New York, NY: Enslow Publishing, 2015.

Sutinis, Beth. *Crime Scene Techs!* Broomall, PA: Mason Crest, 2015.

Websites

American Academy of Forensic Sciences

www.aafs.org

Find more information about what forensic scientists do, the different types of forensic scientists, and programs offered at colleges and universities.

Simon Fraser University, Virtual Museum of Canada, Investigating Forensics

www.sfu.museum/forensics/eng/pg_media-media_pg/anthropologie-anthropology

Learn more about forensic anthropology, watch videos of experts at work, and view photos of the tools and evidence in a forensic lab.

Smithsonian, The Secret in the Cellar: A Written in Bone Forensic Mystery from Colonial America

anthropology.si.edu/writteninbone/comic/XPlayer.html

Play this game to help you learn more about forensic anthropology.

INDEX